Venus AND THE COMETS

by Erika Tamar

Published by Darby Creek Publishing,
a division of Oxford Resources, Inc.
7858 Industrial Parkway
Plain City, OH 43064
www.darbycreekpublishing.com

Cover photography by Michael Petty
Design by Keith Van Norman

Cataloging-in-Publication Data

Tamar, Erika.
Venus and the Comets / by Erika Tamar.
ISBN 1-58196-017-4 / Scholastic Book Fairs Edition
ISBN 1-58196-018-2 / Trade Paperback Edition
p. cm.
Summary: Venus' mother wants her to be a supermodel, but all Venus wants to do is play soccer. When she's scheduled to portray Cinderella at a toy store, Venus has to show everyone what she wants to be.
1. Child models—Juvenile fiction. 2. Soccer players—Juvenile fiction. 3. Identity (Psychology)—Juvenile fiction. [1. Child models—Fiction. 2. Soccer players—Fiction. 3. Identity—Fiction.]
PZ7.T159Ve 2003
[Fic] dd22
OCLC: 52607416

Printed in the United States of America

OPM 10 9 8 7 6 5 4 3 2 1

TABLE OF CONTENTS

CHAPTER ONE

SOCCER BARBIE

"I signed up for soccer," Venus Macguire told her mother.

"You didn't!" The look on Mrs. Macguire's face made Venus's stomach hurt.

"I did."

"You won't!"

"I will!" Venus screamed.

She threw herself on the floor. She kicked her legs. She started her best, biggest tantrum since back when she was five. That was when she didn't get her picture on the Sugar Crunch cereal box. The advertising agency had picked a freckle-faced boy who wasn't half as pretty! And that wasn't fair because Venus Macguire was special. Mom said so.

In most ways, Mrs. Macguire was a nice mother. She was crazy in only one way. Long ago, she had won the Miss Texas Oil Well pageant. She got a big bouquet of roses. She got a little rhinestone oil well to wear on her head. She could never forget that wonderful day. She wanted even more glory for her beautiful daughter. She was training Venus to become The Supermodel of 2013.

"Not soccer!" Mrs. Macguire said. "Venus, you'll get bruises!"

"I don't care!" Venus stamped her feet.

Venus was tired of modeling. She was tired of smiling hard to show her dimples. She was tired of opening her eyes extra-wide to show how gorgeously green they were. She was tired of being tortured by curling irons in her long, red hair. Most of all, she was tired of pretending to be younger than nine. The Cutie-Pie Company said that she'd become too old to model their ruffled little-girl party dresses. Venus wasn't getting many modeling calls anymore.

"You don't have time for soccer," Mrs. Macguire said.

"I do!"

"We should start working on talent, dear, to help you past this . . . uh . . . awkward age." Mrs. Macguire's eyes brightened. "Maybe acting lessons?"

"No, I don't want any," Venus whined.

"You could be the spokesmodel for—for—something," her mother said.

Venus had been the spokesmodel for Little Darling Diapers. She'd lisped, "Oooh, I'm tho dry." That was back when she was three, but the commercial was still on TV—too often! Mom thought it was wonderful, so Venus had bragged about it in school. Now she knew that was a mistake. It was embarrassing to be seen doing the macarena in diapers! The kids in her class teased her whenever the commercial ran. Especially Jill S., Jill M., and Julie.

"One day you could be a supermodel," her mother continued. "You'll be on the runway in designer fashion shows. In Paris, in Italy! Won't that be fun? And on magazine covers, of course. Honestly, Venus, I can see it all now!"

Mrs. Macguire's whole face glowed from

dreaming about it. Mr. Macguire had left long ago, so her attention was all on Venus, her only child. Mrs. Macguire loved everything about Venus's career. A lot more than Venus did. And certainly more than her own career, which was bookkeeping.

Venus's teachers seemed pleased by her sweet model smile and her perfect grooming. But the kids didn't go for it a bit. She didn't even have a best friend. She *had* to find something different to do.

Venus had seen the poster on Main Street. It read: "Pilot Soccer Program. Girls, Age 9. Thursday, September 7, 4:00 P.M., High School Soccer Field." Perfect! She was nine.

Venus thought she might like sports. She'd liked the one ice skating lesson she'd had last year. The instructor told her she was terrific for a beginner. But when she fell, Mom made her quit right away because of the black and blue mark on her leg.

Venus didn't know a thing about soccer. But

she knew it had nothing to do with curling irons. And maybe she could make friends with other nine-year-old girls there. Anyway, the black and white ball was a very attractive design, so soccer might be nice.

Now it was Thursday and she had to get to the soccer field.

"Please get up off the floor, dear," Mrs. Macguire pleaded.

"I want to go to soccer!" Venus held her breath until her face turned blue.

Mrs. Macguire turned pale. As usual, she gave in.

⚽ ⚽ ⚽ ⚽ ⚽

Mom dropped her off. Venus looked around the high school soccer field. Dozens of other nine-year-old girls stood in bunches. They had to be from schools all over town. She wished she knew someone. . . . Oh no! Jill S., Jill M., and Julie from her class were there. They dressed alike and acted alike. Everyone else followed them. They were the most popular girls in fourth grade—and the meanest.

Venus hoped they wouldn't be on her team.

Jill S., Jill M., and Julie each were wearing yellow T-shirts with blue stripes on the sleeves. They had blue shorts with yellow stripes on the sides. They had yellow sweat socks.

Venus's white T-shirt had "Starlet" stitched on it in gold thread. Her white shorts were trimmed with gold ribbon. Her anklets had matching gold edges.

Jill S. saw her first. "Oh look. It's Soccer Barbie!"

Jill M. snorted.

Julie giggled.

Venus wanted to die. How could Mom have been so wrong about her outfit?

A man spoke into a loudspeaker. "Listen up," he said. "When you hear your team number, go to your coach. The coaches are holding up team cards."

"Wait!" a dark-haired girl next to Venus yelled.

"How come we don't get to try out?"

"This is a beginning program," the man answered.

"Yeah!" the girl yelled. "But what about a traveling team? Like an all-star team?"

"Maybe later," the man said. "Okay, everybody. Listen for your numbers. Team One: Mary Hodge, Kelly Donahue, Lisa Cornell . . ."

"I'd make all-star in a second," the dark-haired girl next to Venus muttered, pretending to kick a ball. She was wearing soccer shoes with cleats!

"I guess you've played soccer before," Venus said.

"That's what I *do*." She looked Venus up and down. "You don't look like *you* play."

Venus swallowed hard. "I'm just starting." She tried her best friendly smile. "Uh, what's your name?"

"Carmen Castro. No offense, but I sure hope you're not on *my* team."

Venus turned away and listened for her name.

The man was up to Team Six. "Team Six," he called. "Venus Macguire, Carmen Castro, Jill Swenson, Jill Moore, Julie . . ."

Soccer is a terrible mistake, Venus thought.

CHAPTER TWO

DRIBBLING, DROOLING, OR WORSE

Venus dragged her feet toward the lady with the Number 6 card. Seven other girls were already gathered around her. Carmen Castro looked impatient. Jill S., Jill M., and Julie, all in a row, stared at Venus. Then Julie whispered something and the Jills laughed.

The three Js must have pulled some strings to get on the same team, Venus thought. She wished she could pull strings to make them disappear.

A tall, bony girl, all elbows and knees, gave Venus a shy smile. Her feet, huge in white sneakers, were wildly out of proportion with her matchstick legs. She looked disorganized: her T-shirt half tucked in, one sweat sock pulled high on her calf, the other puddling around her ankle.

Venus smiled back, sort of. She didn't go all-out with her dimples. After all, the girl looked awkward, as if she'd trip over herself, and Mom said clumsy was bad, almost sinful. Still, the girl did have a sweet smile . . .

"Hi," a cute black girl said.

"Hi," Venus answered and stood next to her. The black girl had great big eyes and a little uptilted nose. She was way too short to ever be a supermodel. No competition there. But she was short enough to pass for younger than nine—maybe even for Cutie-Pie ruffles! Venus's body tensed. But wait—this was soccer.

". . . seven . . . eight. Good, we're all here," the lady said.

"There's supposed to be eleven on a team," Carmen said. "And subs."

"This is a practice program, so we're starting off with eight girls and short time periods.

Everyone plays and everyone learns." The lady smiled. "I'm Sue Posner, your coach. This is my daughter Laura Rose."

Laura Rose's hair was dirty-blond. *Needs a few highlights there*, Venus thought.

"Please introduce yourselves," the coach continued.

"Jill S., Jill M., and Julie," they said together.

"Keisha Jefferson," the black girl said.

"Carmen Castro."

"Angie Torelli," the awkward, bony girl said.

"Doesn't your family own Torelli's?" Keisha asked. "My dad takes us there all the time. When he's in town. They have the *best* pasta."

Angie smiled. "And the best tiramisu and the best risotto, too."

Venus's mouth watered. But all those things were *fattening*. Luckily, Venus was naturally thin. She had to stay that way because Mom said the camera added ten pounds. Venus couldn't even remember the last time she'd had real ice cream instead of sorbet . . .

Mrs. Posner was looking at her and waiting.

"Oh. I'm Venus Macguire."

"That's pretty," Keisha said. "Were you named for the planet?"

Venus hesitated. It was too embarrassing to admit she was named for the Goddess of Love and Beauty. "That's right, the planet," she mumbled.

"Why didn't they name you Pluto?" Jill S. said with a sneer. Jill M. and Julie laughed meanly.

Carmen frowned at them. "Ease up, we're supposed to be *teammates.*"

"Right," Keisha said. "My dad says team spirit counts for a whole lot."

Carmen and Keisha are okay, Venus thought, *but what is this team thing? Are we supposed to love each other or something? Even clumsy people with enormous duck feet?*

"Who's played soccer before?" Mrs. Posner asked.

"Me!" Carmen said. "My parents came from Colombia where soccer's like the national sport. My brothers play in the county league." Carmen had a big, happy smile. "I love soccer! I can juggle twenty times and do headers."

"Sounds terrific," Mrs. Posner said, "though we don't encourage headers for beginning teams."

"We've played before," Jill S., Jill M., and Julie said.

"I haven't," Keisha said, "but it looks like fun. You don't have to be that tall for soccer, do you?"

"Wait, now I remember," Angie said. "Isn't your dad Ray Jefferson?"

"Uh-huh. I guess I take after my mom. She's petite."

"*Ray Jefferson!*" the two Jills said. "Wow!"

"Who's Ray Jefferson?" Venus asked.

"Don't you know *anything?*" Carmen shook her head. "He's only MVP on the Knicks."

"Oh," Venus said.

Angie caught her blank look. "Most Valuable Player. Basketball," she whispered.

"Thanks," Venus whispered back.

"Don't feel bad," Angie whispered. "I wouldn't know either, if he didn't come into our restaurant."

Angie is nice, Venus decided. Sometimes Mom was wrong about things.

"How about the rest of you?" Mrs. Posner asked.

Angie hung her head. "I've never played much sports."

"Me either," Venus said, "but Angie and I can learn, can't we? " She sounded lots braver than she felt.

Mrs. Posner nodded. "That's exactly what we're here for."

"I've only kicked a ball around the backyard," Laura Rose said. "My mom's going to teach us the rules."

"Well, let's talk about the basics," Mrs. Posner said. "You score by kicking the ball into the other team's goal. The team is divided into forwards or offense, midfielders, and defense. The goalie stays in front of the goal and you . . ."

Offense? Venus thought. Offensive meant rude, didn't it? The two Jills and Julie would be excellent at that. But what was the offense supposed to do?

Yell insults at the other team?

". . . you have to play your positions," Mrs. Posner continued. "The defense helps to protect the goal and passes to the midfielders. Midfielders pass to the forwards, and the forwards go for the goal. The point is to move the ball to the other team's end. You move the ball with your feet. You can use your head, too, or knees, but no hands. Except for the goalie."

"When do we have games?" Carmen asked.

"Every Saturday, starting in two weeks," Mrs. Posner said. "Our first game will be September twenty-third. We'll play Team Five."

"But we're not ready! We've never even played together," Jill M. said, "and some people . . . ," she glared at Venus, ". . . some people wouldn't know a soccer ball if it came up and bit them!"

"Beginners will learn by playing," Mrs. Posner said, "and the experienced players can help them. Don't worry. The other teams have a mix of skills, too. Today we'll work on dribbling and . . ."

Don't worry? Venus *was* worried. She liked to be the best—but she didn't understand a thing about soccer!

"Can we have a team name?" Keisha was hopping with excitement.

"Sure," Mrs. Posner said, smiling. "Any ideas?"

Everyone started calling out ideas.

"The Sharks!"

"The Blasters!"

"The Kickers!"

"The Starlets?" Venus suggested.

Jill S. pantomimed her finger down her throat as Jill M. said, "Yuk."

"The Comets!" Carmen said, "'Cause we'll be so fast and fiery!"

"Yeah, the Comets!"

"Let's go, Comets," Mrs. Posner said. "Warm-ups first. Twenty sit-ups, twenty jumping-jacks."

No problem, Venus thought, *I can do a million sit-ups.* Mom made her do them every morning. They were supposed to keep her tummy flat. Even so, she had to remember to hold it in when the photographers looked her over.

". . . five . . . six . . . seven . . . eight . . . ," Mrs. Posner counted.

Carmen was breezing through them, too. But Angie was gasping. She had to be way out of shape.

". . . fourteen . . . fifteen . . . sixteen . . ."

Okay so far, Venus thought. Her head was buzzing with "juggling," "header," "goalie." It was all a mystery. "Dribbling." That sounded disgusting, like drooling—or worse!

Doing twenty jumping jacks was no problem, either. Venus's long, red curls bounced against her shoulders. She had strong legs. Leg exercises were in her morning routine because muscles made curves. Mom said that photographers didn't like straight, skinny legs.

Keisha was jumping pretty high for such a short kid. Angie hardly got off the ground. She seemed to have a problem getting her legs and arms to work together. Her face was bright red. She looked like she wanted to cry.

Venus knew how she felt. Her own face would be bright red once practice started. Jill S., Jill M., and Julie would get everyone to laugh at her. And Jill S., Jill M., and Julie would tell everyone at school.

Venus wished the warm-ups would last forever.

CHAPTER THREE

POWER KICK

Mrs. Posner stood in front of the net.

"Line up, girls," she said. "Dribble part way and then kick it in."

Carmen rushed to the head of the line. Venus went to the very end. Angie got behind her. Venus left the line. She pretended to tie her shoe. Then she went behind Angie. Good, she was last again. In school or at an audition, she'd always push to the front. She liked to be first for everything. But now she didn't want a turn at all.

"Carmen, show them," Mrs. Posner said.

Carmen moved the black and white ball forward, passing it from one foot to the other. Then her kick sent it whizzing straight into the goal.

"Good!" Mrs. Posner said. "Everybody, see how Carmen used the inside of her foot to dribble?"

Keisha was next. The ball kept getting ahead of her, and she ran to catch up to it.

"The *inside* of your foot," Mrs. Posner said. "Control that ball."

"But, Coach, it's faster if I keep kicking it in front of me," Keisha said.

"That's fine if you've got a breakaway. Otherwise, it's too easy for the other team to take it from you."

What's a breakaway? Venus wondered.

"What's a breakaway?" Angie asked.

Good, someone's asking, Venus thought.

"That's when you've broken away from the pack. You have a clear field ahead, with no interference to worry about. Then you can kick the ball ahead of you and run with it."

Keisha tried again. The ball kept getting away from her. "Carmen made it look so *easy*," she said when she came back to the line.

"You don't even know how hard I work,"

Carmen responded. "I'm always tagging along with my brothers for practices." Carmen grinned. "I make them crazy!"

Jill S. dribbled well. But when she kicked, the ball hit the post and bounced back.

"It feels more natural to kick with your toe," the coach said. "But kick with the top of your foot instead. Get your shoelaces under it. That lets you aim better."

Dribble, inside of foot, shoelaces, Venus thought. She bit her lip.

Jill M. went, then Julie, then Laura Rose.

Now only Angie was ahead of her. *Let's have a thunderstorm right now,* Venus prayed. *With lots of lightning.* Then she could go home and forget all about the Comets.

The sun kept shining. Angie tried to dribble. She tripped over her feet. Her kick died short of the net.

"Good try," Mrs. Posner said.

Angie looked miserable.

"Good try," Venus whispered as Angie came

back to the line. She felt sorry for her. Venus felt even more sorry for herself.

Venus followed Angie to the end of the line. She bent down and pretended to fix her socks. If she knelt down real low behind Angie, maybe Mrs. Posner wouldn't notice her.

"Come on, Venus!" the coach called.

Venus took a big breath. Everyone was waiting and watching.

Okay. She took another breath.

"What're you waiting for?" Jill M. yelled. "You want a special invitation?"

"Leave her alone," Angie said. "She's getting ready."

Venus gave Angie a quick, grateful look. No one in school had ever stuck up for her.

There's no way out of this, Venus thought. *Here goes.*

She tapped the ball from her inside left foot to her right, and back again. And then again. Maybe it wasn't that impossible—

"Hey, Venus! You're supposed to move it *forward!*" Jill S. yelled. Jill M. and Julie giggled.

Venus blushed. She'd been trying so hard that she hadn't realized—she was dribbling in place!

"That's okay. You're getting the hang of it," Mrs. Posner called.

Venus inched the ball forward a little and then some more. She got it moving faster. She lost it once, but got it back almost right away. Not that bad. *Now for the kick.* She looked ahead at the goal and thought, *Get my shoelaces under and*— She let go.

A black and white blur sailed over Mrs. Posner, over the goal, far over the field to where other teams were practicing.

"Oops, sorry," Venus mumbled. No one else had kicked the ball that far away. She was the team dunce.

"That's some power kick!" Mrs. Posner said, laughing. "Once you get that under control, you'll be fine."

Everyone was looking at her like she'd done something good!

Carmen raised her left eyebrow. "You're sure

you never played soccer before?"

Venus shook her head.

"You must be some kind of natural," Carmen said. "Funny, I never would have expected you to . . . I mean, the way you look . . . You really *booted* it!"

Carmen was surprised, but Venus was amazed! Happy. No, downright thrilled. Imagine that! She was a soccer natural!

Sunshine warmed her arms. The grass smelled fresh.

Jill M.'s voice broke through her good feelings. "You're supposed to go get the ball, Pluto."

"No, she's too bee-*yoo*-ti-ful," Julie said. "Look, she's waiting for a slave to get it for her."

She'd forgotten all about the ball. Venus felt stung. True, in school she always got one of the boys to do things for her. Especially yucky things, like cleaning the guinea pig's cage.

Venus ran far across the field to the ball. She was about to scoop it up. Then she changed her mind. She kicked it hard. There was a good loud *thwack*. The ball flew all the way back to Mrs. Posner.

That first kick wasn't just a fluke! This was something she could do!

CHAPTER FOUR

TEAMMATE TALK

"Now let's work on passing," Mrs. Posner said.

Venus brushed her red curls away from her eyes. She wished she had a headband like Carmen's to pull them back. But they'd look less gorgeous that way.

"When you pass to a teammate, you aim the ball right at her feet. When you get the ball, trap it. You don't want to give the other team a chance to steal it away."

The coach tossed three more balls onto the grass. "Break up into pairs and keep passing to each other as you move up the field."

The Three Js scrambled to be next to each other.

Mrs. Posner looked at them. "Into *pairs*."

"Can't the three of us stay together?" Jill S. whined.

"No," Mrs. Posner said. "Let's go, girls. Julie—with Venus."

Julie groaned out loud. "Oh no, not *her!*" She stomped over to Venus.

Venus's face turned red. She took a moment to adjust the ball at her feet.

"So pass it," Julie muttered. "Like, whenever you're ready."

Venus kicked the ball right at Julie's sneering face.

Julie managed to get her forehead under it and return it. A header! Darn it, she was good.

This time Venus aimed for her stomach.

Julie kneed it back. It sailed way past Venus, and she glared at Julie.

"Go get it, *prima donna*," Julie said.

Venus ran for the ball. She wasn't sure what "prima donna" meant. But she knew it couldn't be anything good. She booted it way over Julie's head.

Let *Julie* run for it this time!

The other girls managed to move in close pairs, but Venus and Julie were all over the field.

Mrs. Posner came over. “Excellent use of your head and knees, Julie. And you’ve got a great power kick, Venus. But for now, how about using only feet, slow and controlled? The point is to make it *easy* for your teammate to receive the ball.”

“Okay,” Julie muttered.

“Okay,” Venus mumbled.

They got into the rhythm of trapping and passing, trapping and passing. They glared at each other all the way down the field.

“Why did I have to get stuck with the Diaper Princess?” Julie said under her breath.

“You always need the Jills to hold your hand,” Venus said back. “You can’t make one single move without them!”

Julie’s eyes widened. “I hate you, Venus Macguire,” she said as she passed the ball.

“You hate me just because I’m beautiful,” Venus said as she trapped it.

"Yeah, right. No, it's 'cause you're a self-centered, spoiled brat."

"You're jealous, that's all," Venus answered. Mom always said the other kids were jealous of her.

"Why should I be?"

Venus kicked the ball to Julie's feet. "Because *I'm* in the ad for Chewy-Chew Bubble Gum and *you're* not."

"You've got a big swelled head! How do you get your T-shirt over it?"

"And I get a year's supply of free Chewy-Chew!"

"I hope you choke on it," Julie said.

Venus trapped the ball. She stood there and tried to think of a snappy answer.

Mrs. Posner blew her whistle.

Everyone stopped.

"I want you to watch how well Julie and Venus work together. They were *talking* to each other. Remember, you can talk to each other out there. *Communicate* with your teammates. Okay, Venus and Julie, show them."

Venus and Julie looked at each other. Julie's mouth twitched as if she was trying not to laugh.

They began to trap and pass, trap and pass, up the field.

"We're supposed to be talking," Julie whispered.

"What are we supposed to say?" Venus asked. She felt strange with everyone watching.

Julie trapped the ball. "For you, Venus," she said loudly as she passed it.

Venus got her foot on it. "Back to you," she called.

"Head's up, Venus. Here it comes."

"Julie! To you!"

"Get it, Venus!"

Julie looked like she was holding in a fit of giggles. By the time the girls came to the end of the field, they were both laughing. They ran back to the rest of the team.

Jill M. looked at Julie suspiciously.

Jill S. frowned. "Why were you joking around with *her?*"

"I wasn't!" Julie said quickly.

"Jill-clone," Venus muttered.

"It sure looked like you were," Jill S. said.

"Well, I wasn't, okay?" Julie glanced at Venus. She shrugged. "Anyway, she's not that bad."

Coming from Julie, Venus thought, *that means I must be doing great!*

CHAPTER FIVE

STEALING THE BALL

"Let's play keep-away," Mrs. Posner said. "Everyone, pair up with a different partner this time. Pretend your partner's on the *other* team. Try to steal the ball and keep it away from her. No tripping, no hands, no pushing."

Venus was paired with Carmen this time.

"A sliding tackle is legal," Mrs. Posner continued. "Show them, Carmen. Take the ball away from me."

Carmen hesitated. "You want me to tackle you, Coach?"

"Sure. Come on."

"Mrs. P is so cool," Keisha whispered.

Mrs. Posner started dribbling the ball. Carmen ran after her and, in one sweeping move, she slid her feet under Mrs. Posner's. They both hit the ground.

This can get rough, Venus thought. She never did rough things. *Maybe I can play without falling down and getting dirty,* she thought.

The coach scrambled to her feet. "Nice job, Carmen. See, girls, the other player is taken by surprise and knocked off balance, so you can steal the ball. The problem is you go down, too. You have to get up fast." She brushed grass from her shorts.

Each pair of girls placed a ball between them. Venus looked at Carmen. Carmen's eyes narrowed. She looked tough. Anyone could see that Carmen was the star of this team. At least so far. Venus's eyes narrowed, too. After all, she'd elbow other models out of the way if she had to. She'd do *anything* to get the job.

"All right, on the whistle!"

Venus went for the ball before Mrs. Posner had even puckered her lips. But Carmen got it away in a flash.

Venus ran after her. Carmen dribbled the ball this way and that. When Venus came close, Carmen turned and was off in a different direction. She was too good!

Venus had to *win*. She tightened her jaw. She pulled a burst of speed from somewhere deep inside. For a moment, Carmen let the ball get a bit away from her. That was Venus's chance! She stole the ball from just in front of Carmen's feet. She kicked it ahead, and they both ran for it at top speed. Carmen got it first. She was fast!

Venus followed close behind, gasping. She had to get that ball. She had to be number one! This was an emergency! She threw herself toward the ground and slid her feet under Carmen's. In one second both girls were lying on the grass. The sliding tackle worked! Carmen was startled. That gave Venus a chance to get up fast and steal the ball.

She was dribbling it down the field when the whistle blew.

The team jogged back to Mrs. Posner. Venus was sweating. Her curls hung in wet tangles. She had scraped her knee. She was panting with her mouth wide open. She knew that didn't look beautiful. But she'd taken the ball away from Carmen! She couldn't believe she had done a tackle.

Oh great! Now Carmen would hate her, too!

"Are you mad?" Venus whispered.

Carmen looked at her as if she had two heads. "You kidding? We're teammates," she said. "That was good practice."

"You mean you're *not* mad at me?" Venus asked.

"You caught me by surprise, that's all. You're kind of . . . competitive."

"I'm sorry," Venus said.

"What for? Hey, that's good for the team."

The team, Venus thought. She wouldn't be competing all by herself, just for herself, like at the auditions. Sometimes that felt lonely. But this—this was something brand new.

But Venus couldn't help it. She still wanted to be the star of the Comets!

CHAPTER SIX

A FRIEND

"One last thing for today," Mrs. Posner said. "Everyone, once around the track."

The girls groaned and moaned.

"Come on, Comets. Running is the best exercise for soccer." The coach led the way to the high school track at the end of the field.

Carmen skipped ahead.

Venus walked next to Angie. Angie's T-shirt was wet. She was pulling at it where it stuck to her.

"Um—I don't run much," Angie mumbled.

"Not even at recess?" Venus asked.

"No. Well, I'm not fast. I stumble a lot. My shoelaces get untied. I don't know how that happens. They just untie themselves, even when I doubleknot them! Some of the kids make fun of me. And I'm no good at catching either." Angie bit her lower lip. "I'm always the very last one picked for teams, so I don't play sports that much."

"Oh." Venus tried to think of something encouraging to say. "I know how you feel. I don't have anyone to play with at recess, either. Everyone at my school hates me, too."

Angie looked surprised. "*Everyone* doesn't hate me. Just a bunch of mean kids."

"Oh."

"My mom says I'm just at an awkward stage, and I'll grow into my body. And my dad says it's what's in your heart that counts. I try to be kind and helpful. I think I have a good heart," Angie continued.

"You do," Venus said. "I could tell right away."

"Venus, why are the three Js so nasty to you?"

"I don't know," Venus answered.

"I don't get it. You're really *nice!*"

Was she? She was beautiful for sure, Venus knew. And she was a successful model. At least she used to be when she was younger and cuddlier. That should make the kids in school *admire* her. Mom said so. But they didn't.

"I don't think I'll run," Angie said. "I'll be way behind everyone and they might make fun of me . . . You go ahead."

"No, this is different," Venus said. "We're a team. No one'll make fun of a teammate." She hoped that was true. She thought Carmen felt that way. But Jill M., Jill S., and Julie were probably busy thinking up new Venus cracks.

"I guess I'll try." But Angie was walking slower and slower. Venus could tell she didn't want to reach the track.

"Come on, Angie. I'll jog with you the whole way around."

At the track, Carmen speeded ahead. Venus was dying to take off. But she had promised. She stayed far back with Angie. Boy, she'd never done *that* for anyone before!

"How come you signed up for soccer?" Venus asked.

Angie was puffing. She could hardly talk. "My parents don't want me to be a couch potato. They said I had to do ballet or soccer or something."

Venus didn't even want to think about Angie doing pirouettes!

"I think soccer will be fun," Venus said.

"Anyway, I'm not quitting. I'm going to hang in and do my best."

"Me, too," Venus said.

"I'm going to practice," Angie said. "I am." She was huffing and puffing. "I'm going to practice running, too."

She's brave, Venus thought, *and easy to talk to.* Maybe Angie could be her friend. "You know what? I'll run with you. If you want to, we can meet at the track every day after school, okay?" Maybe they'd even do other things together, like sleepovers and whatever else friends did.

"That would be great! But let's do it late, when there's not too many people at the track to see me," Angie said.

"Okay. They say if you work hard at something,

you have to get better at it," Venus said. "Sports or schoolwork or anything."

No, wait. That's not true about modeling, Venus thought. It mostly depended on the tilt of your nose. Or the color of your eyes. Or whatever the ad people wanted that day. There was nothing to practice. But now, with soccer, it *was* up to her. She liked that. She could work extra-hard to become as good as Carmen.

A few minutes later, the Comets flopped down on the grass in front of Mrs. Posner.

"Mrs. P is so nice, isn't she?" Angie whispered. "My sister's swim team coach screams and yells at the team all the time. Gina thinks he's just in it for his own glory."

"I like Mrs. P," Venus whispered back.

"Another thing—she doesn't treat Laura Rose any different. She's fair," Angie said.

"How do you mean?

"She doesn't shove her own daughter in front of everybody else," Angie said. "A lot of other coaches would."

Mom sure would, Venus thought. It had to be nice for Laura Rose to have a mother who wasn't pushing her. Of course, Mom did all those things for Venus, but maybe a little bit was for her own glory, too. That was a bad thought, and Venus brushed it away. But she couldn't help wishing Mom was more like Mrs. Posner.

"That was a good practice," the coach said. "Now listen up. You have two weeks to get what you'll need for the game. Shin guards under your socks, and if possible, soccer cleats. Not football cleats. They're illegal. If you can get your equipment sooner, that's great—but be sure to have it for Saturday the twenty-third."

"When's our next practice?" Julie asked.

"After school Monday. Please be here at four sharp for warm-ups."

"Okay, Coach," Jill S. said.

"So—are we going to be the best team ever?" Mrs. Posner asked.

"Comets number one!" Carmen yelled.

"Number one!" Laura Rose yelled.

"Number one!" Venus echoed.

They gave each other high-fives.

Mrs. Posner looked at her watch. "That's it for today."

Venus started off the field. Suddenly she realized she was walking all alone. She looked over her shoulder. Some of the girls were helping Mrs. Posner move the goals. Others were picking up balls.

Venus ran back. She grabbed a ball that had bounced away. She put it in the big mesh bag.

She could feel Julie watching her.

CHAPTER SEVEN

SPOILED BRAT

"Your beautiful white outfit!" Mom was driving Venus home from practice. "I can't believe this! You looked gorgeous when you left the house."

"Mom, watch the road!"

"Your knee!" Mom said. "It's a disaster!"

The blood on Venus's knee had dried to brown. It was streaked with dirt.

"It's okay," Venus said. "It doesn't hurt much."

Mom stopped for a red light. She turned to stare at Venus. "Just look at yourself!"

Venus's white shorts had grass stains. A bit of the gold ribbon dangled from them. A black smudge covered the *l* on her "Starlet" T-shirt. And her lovely hair was stiff with dried sweat.

"What in the world were you doing?" Mom asked.

"Playing soccer," Venus said. "And guess what? Somebody said I'm a natural! Well, not as good as Carmen—not yet. Oh, yeah, Mom, I need sweat socks and shin guards and cleats and—"

"*Sweat* socks? *Cleats?*" Mom sounded as though Venus were asking for an Uzi. "Do you really plan to go on with this?"

"Mom, I can't wait 'til Saturday. Saturday, September twenty-third!"

"I know, it'll be exciting." Then Mom looked at Venus's scrape and frowned. "We'll have to cover up that knee somehow. Maybe it'll heal by then. Oh, well, if it doesn't, make-up should take care of it—"

"I don't need *make-up*," Venus said. "I could use a bandage, I guess."

"A bandage? For *Saturday?*"

"Oh, and I want a sweatband and—"

"You can't appear at the opening with a bandage," Mom said.

"It won't get in my way—Wait. *What* opening?"

"The OH BOY! TOYS! opening in Mineola. On Saturday, the twenty-third!"

"*That* Saturday?" Venus groaned. "I forgot." Mom always arranged those things for her. How was she supposed to remember?

"You're the Cinderella doll." Mom smiled. "You'll cut the ribbon and be photographed."

"I can't, Mom."

"OH BOY! is a very big chain, honey. When they see you at the opening, maybe they'll want you for their commercials!"

"Mom, I've got a game!"

"What game?"

"The Comets! It's our first game. It's really important!"

"OH BOY! TOYS!—now *that's* important."

"I'm playing soccer that Saturday!"

"No, you're not!"

"Yes, I am! I am! I am!"

⚽ ⚽ ⚽ ⚽ ⚽

There was an awful silence at dinner that night. Mom pushed the stringbeans around on her plate. Venus couldn't swallow a thing.

Finally Mom spoke. "It's a wonderful opportunity, Venus. The president of OH BOY! will be there."

"I don't want to cut their dumb ribbon!"

Venus remembered the last time she was hired for an opening. It was for the new Wiener World on Northern Boulevard. She had to wear a potato chip costume. It itched. She stood next to a man dressed as a hot dog. There were balloons and streamers—but no one came. No one. It felt really stupid to cut the ribbon in an empty parking lot.

"It'll be like Wiener World," Venus mumbled.

"All right, that was a mistake," Mom said.

"This is different. This is *big*. This could jumpstart your career."

"I don't want my career."

Another long silence.

"Mom, I like soccer."

"You must be joking."

"I like it! It's something I can *do*. I'm *good* at it."

"You're good at modeling. And I've worked very hard to make sure you have all the opportunities I missed."

Venus knew the tricks. She put glycerine on her teeth so her lips didn't stick when she had to smile and smile. She knew how to pretend to be seven or eleven. When they asked her how old she was, she knew enough to say "How old do you need?"

Once she'd lost a job because she was too beautiful. They'd wanted a regular kid. She had *tried* to act like a regular kid. She had talked to the ad people about riding a bike and playing with her dog,

Ruffian. Even though she'd never had a dog.

She didn't want to smile and pretend anymore.

"This thing with the Meteors—" Mom began.

"*Comets.*"

"Whatever. You'll have to get over it."

"I won't!"

"Don't be silly. What about the beautiful Cinderella dress? And the pretty glass slippers?"

"*Glass!* You want me to walk on *glass?*"

"Okay, plastic. But they're lovely. You'll wear them on Saturday and—"

"I'll wear them for Halloween!"

"Venus Macguire, stop acting like a spoiled brat!"

Kids in school called her a spoiled brat. Julie and the Jills and a lot of people did. Now her own mother!

"Well, *you're* the one who spoiled me!" Venus ran upstairs to her room.

She could hear Mom downstairs.

This was too hard.

Mom was slamming silverware into the sink.

Venus blinked back tears. She had a feeling that turning blue wouldn't help this time.

CHAPTER EIGHT

THE TERRIBLE Js

In school on Friday morning, the Jills and Julie told everyone about the soccer program. The Terrible Js were excited about it.

"We're Comets!" Julie said.

"Comets rule!" Jill M. and Jill S. said together.

They all slapped hands.

Venus felt left out. And mad. They acted like she wasn't even on the team.

At least for today, she was still a Comet.

Venus wished a tornado would whisk OH BOY! TOYS! into the sky. Or that a big flood would come and make it float far, far away.

She had to think of some way out.

She could pretend to be sick that Saturday.

That's what she'd do! She'd run hot water over the thermometer and—no, that wouldn't work. If she was sick, Mom wouldn't let her go to soccer either.

If she kept acting like a Comet and practicing like a Comet, maybe somehow she would remain a Comet. Maybe some kind of magic would work for her. She just *had* to be in the first game!

Venus thought about recess. She knew two soccer balls were in the equipment room. The boys had dibs on one of them. She'd bet anything that Julie and the Jills would grab the other. And they'd never let her play with them. Normally, Venus didn't do much at recess, maybe comb her long hair and redo her lip gloss. Getting sweaty and dirty wasn't her style. But today she wanted to practice soccer!

Recess was right after lunch. Venus ate extra-fast. Then she went up to the cafeteria teacher and smiled her sweetest, most dimply smile. "May I be excused, Ms. Leeds?" Venus asked. "I want to go to the girls' room."

The teacher hesitated. "Lunch is almost over.

Perhaps you could wait a few minutes?"

"But I want to go *now*."

Venus got permission. She knew she would. She went straight to the equipment room. She was the first one there. When everyone else came out to the school yard, Venus was already clutching the soccer ball.

Julie and the Jills looked furious.

Venus decided to juggle the ball from knee to knee the way Carmen did. She couldn't do it very well. The ball bounced away from her. Jill S. ran to grab it, but Venus managed to pick it up fast.

"Stop hogging the ball," Jill M. said.

"I had it first," Venus answered.

"Yeah, you have to be *first* for everything," Julie said.

"Oink, oink," Jill S. said.

"Selfish!" Jill M. said.

Venus kept trying to juggle. Julie and the Jills crossed their arms and watched her.

Playing soccer all by herself wasn't much fun. She heard the shouts of other kids running and playing on the field. It made her feel lonely. She wished Carmen, Angie, Keisha, and Laura Rose went to her school.

Venus dribbled the ball from foot to foot. She was very careful to keep it from rolling away toward Julie and the Jills. She knew they'd run off with it if they had a chance.

Jill M. tapped her foot impatiently. "You want to jump rope instead?" she asked the other Js.

"No," Jill S. answered.

"This is a waste of recess!" Julie exclaimed.

"We have a game coming up," Jill said. "We've got to practice."

"For the good of the Comets," Julie added. She glared at Venus.

Venus held the ball tight in her arms.

"We're on the same team," she said.

"Duh! Like we don't know," Jill S. said.

"Unfortunately," Jill M. said.

Venus took a breath. "So if you guys want to play keep-away . . ."

Julie and the Jills looked at each other.

"Keep-away works better with four," Julie finally said. "We could break up, two against two."

Jill M. rolled her eyes. "But who's gonna be with *her?*"

"Not me!" Jill S. said.

"All right, I will," Julie said. "Come on, let's go, recess is half over!"

Julie and Venus teamed up against the Jills. They kicked and ran all over the field. Venus tripped and scraped her knee in the exact same place. Mom would be mad, but she didn't care. It was so much better to *play* at recess! It was lots better than just sitting somewhere looking beautiful in her beautiful dresses.

Jill M. was kicking the ball in front of her. She was getting away from everybody. Venus ran her fastest and caught up. She stole the ball away.

"Okay!" Julie yelled. She gave Venus a high-five. Then Julie looked startled by what she had done. But it made Venus feel happy anyway.

If only she didn't have to think about OH BOY! TOYS!

CHAPTER NINE

MAKING THE CUT

For two weeks Mom talked about Cinderella and the opening. For two weeks, Venus went to soccer practice on Mondays and Thursdays. Mrs. Posner set up pairs of cones on the field. The girls had to kick the ball one at a time, aiming for the space between the cones.

"The coach said my aim's getting better," Venus told Mom, "but I need to work on it." She could see that Mom wasn't the least bit interested.

Soon it was Saturday, September 23rd—game day!

That Saturday morning, Venus stayed in bed until late. She was supposed to be getting her beauty sleep. But she lay wide-awake, thinking.

She still didn't have cleats. Or shin guards. Nothing had changed. Mom was going to *make* her go to OH BOY! TOYS! Venus didn't get out of bed until Mom called her down for brunch.

Venus nibbled at a slice of toast. She was too miserable to be hungry.

"Finish up," Mom said. "You're having your hair done at one."

Venus pushed away the crusts. "I'm through."

"All right, get dressed. We have to leave soon."

Venus clomped up the stairs and slammed into her room.

She stared into the mirror over her dresser. How could she smile today? The Comets would be running and kicking without her.

"Are you getting ready?" Mom called from downstairs. "Are you brushing your teeth?"

That would be with the extra-super-white toothpaste. Venus decided to skip it. But unbrushed teeth wasn't enough to save her from OH BOY! TOYS! It would take something *big*. Something . . .

"Hurry up, Venus!"

Venus opened the closet. There hung the Cinderella dress. It was pink satin with a million sequins. The skirt ballooned over scratchy petticoats. Mom would wrap it in plastic and hang it in the car. She'd help Venus put it on at the last minute. After make-up.

Venus went to the dresser. She took the scissors out of the top drawer.

She walked back to the closet. She stared at the dress. She opened the scissors and grabbed a handful of the material and—

She couldn't do it. That dress had to be so expensive. OH BOY! TOYS! might make Mom pay for it.

Back to the dresser. She looked at herself in the mirror. The scissors were still in her hand. She raised them. She cut the first chunk of hair near her ear. Soon other chunks fell. The scissors made a swoosh-swoosh sound as they chopped faster and faster.

Red ringlets dropped from her shoulders. They

piled up on the floor.

She felt as if she were in a dream.

The sound of the door opening startled her.

"Venus, what's taking you so— Oh! oh! oh, Venus!"

"Mom, I—"

"Oh!" Mom walked toward Venus. She stepped on long, reddish curls. She looked down at them. "Oh!" Her eyes filled with tears.

A big, terrible lump swelled in Venus's throat.

"Oh, Venus! Your beautiful hair!"

"Mom." Venus reached out for her. "Mom, I'm sorry," she whispered.

Mom sobbed out loud. She took Venus's hand and held on tight.

Seeing Mom cry scared Venus. What had she done? Her eyes filled.

"How could you?" Mom sobbed.

"I didn't mean to," Venus wailed. Rivers of tears ran down her cheeks.

"But why?"

"I don't know. It just happened. I don't know."

There was a long, terrible silence. The only sound in the room was the ticking of the clock.

Mom brushed the tears from her eyes. "Did you hate going to OH BOY! *that much?*" Her voice was hoarse.

"I don't know." Venus swallowed hard. "I guess . . . I guess I wanted *soccer* that much."

"Soccer? I didn't think you . . . I didn't know it was that . . ." Mom fingered the hair that was left on Venus's head. "It'll be all right. It's not so . . . um . . ."

"Oh, Mommy."

"Okay, honey. It's okay."

Mom put her arms around Venus. They hugged and they cried together.

"All right." Mom pulled herself together. "I guess I didn't understand. All right, you won't be Cinderella. So long, Fairy Godmother." Mom tried to smile, but she couldn't quite do it. "You didn't really want any of that, did you?"

She went into the bathroom. Venus heard the water running. She heard lots of splashing.

Venus made herself look in the mirror. Her hair was very short on one side. Funny tufts poked up on top.

Mom came back into the room. She was patting her face with a towel. "Well, that's better," she said in a shaky voice. Her eyes were still red. "I thought . . . I thought we both wanted the same thing. Why didn't you tell me?"

"I did," Venus said. "I tried."

"Did I forget to listen?" Mom bit her lip. "I'm sorry."

"Hair grows—doesn't it?" Venus whispered.

"I'll call . . . I know someone who'll—" Mom said. "What time is it? We'll get it . . . uh . . . styled later this afternoon."

"Does that mean I can go to my soccer game?" Venus's voice came out very tiny.

"Your game." Mom blew her nose. She took a long, shuddery breath. "When is it?"

"Warm-ups are at two-thirty sharp." Venus sniffled and wiped her cheeks.

"Okay, warm-ups. Oh, it's almost one-thirty!" All that crying had taken a long time.

"Is it too late?" Venus asked.

"We have just enough time to go to the store. Hurry, wash your face."

"Mom?"

"I'll bandage your knee. We'll get those things you need. Those cliffs and—"

"Cleats."

"But your hair will have to wait."

"I guess it has to."

No matter what, Venus was going to the game! But could she play soccer with a paper bag over her head?

CHAPTER TEN

WARM-UPS

With all the rushing, Venus got to to the field early. Only Julie was there. She wished Julie wasn't the first person she had to face. At least Jill M. and Jill S. hadn't come yet.

Venus had new sweat socks. She had shin guards and cleats. Best of all, she was wearing an athletic T-shirt and shorts like the other girls had. She had a new blue sweatband. It would have held the hair out of her face. If she had hair to hold back. She hoped the band was covering the funny tufts on top. She thought maybe she didn't look *that* bad. Until she saw Julie's face.

"Whoa!" Julie said. "What happened to you?"

Venus turned away.

"Looks like you were attacked by a pair of scissors."

Venus shrugged.

"You cut it yourself, didn't you?"

"Sort of." Venus looked down. She wished Julie would leave her alone.

"Oh boy," Julie said. "I did that to myself in first grade."

"Really?"

"Why did you do yours?" Julie asked.

"It's a long story," Venus mumbled.

"I like long stories."

Julie waited. Venus didn't say anything.

"I cut mine because my mom and dad were getting a divorce," Julie continued. "I don't know what I was thinking. It didn't help anything." She shrugged. "Anyway, it grew back."

Venus envied Julie's ponytail.

"My mom took me to this place. They knew how to fix it—well, at least even it out. You want me to get the address for you?"

"My mom knows places to go," Venus said.

Jill S. and Jill M. appeared on the field. "Hey, Julie! Come on!"

Julie hesitated and then she ran toward them.

Venus watched her go. Julie was being nice to her—for a minute anyway. What was *that* all about?

Mrs. Posner and Laura Rose arrived. Then the other Comets. There wasn't much of a chance to talk about her hair. Venus was glad. They were busy putting on the orange pinnies that Mrs. Posner handed out.

Team Five was across the field. They were putting on blue pinnies.

It was time for warm-ups. Some parents had already collected at the edge of the field to watch the game. Venus was half-nervous and half-excited. A real game, with an audience! Mom had dropped her off. She still wasn't interested in soccer.

"For today, Venus and Carmen, forwards," Mrs. Posner said. "Laura Rose and Jill S., midfield. Julie, Jill M., and Keisha, defense. Angie in goal.

I'll rotate positions for other games, so you'll all have a chance at everything."

"The other guys are supposed to pass up to us," Carmen said to Venus. "We'll be the ones going for goals."

It was a responsibility, Venus thought. Scoring for the Comets will be so great!

"The most important thing, " Mrs. Posner said. "You've got to play your positions. That separates a good team from a bad one. I don't want to see you all running together in a big clump. Okay?"

"Okay!" the Comets said.

They did their stretches. They started their sit-ups. They checked out Team Five across the field. They were doing warm-ups, too.

"They look strong," Keisha said.

"They look rough," Laura Rose said.

"And tough," Angie added.

"No tougher than us!" Carmen said. "The Comets rule!"

More parents collected at the sidelines. Venus saw Carmen wave at a middle-aged couple with three teenage boys. They had to be her soccer-playing brothers. When a very tall black man and a petite black lady appeared, there was the kind of buzz that celebrities get. Venus thought, *He has to be Ray Jefferson.*

"He came!" Keisha was bubbling. "I didn't think he'd make it. He's supposed to do a personal appearance someplace. But he came!"

"Get 'em, Angie!" a man's voice yelled.

"That's my dad." Angie smiled through her blush.

A lonely feeling swept over Venus.

"Let's go, Comets," Mrs. Posner called.

Venus's breath came fast. She was ready—she hoped! She and the Comets ran onto the field.

CHAPTER ELEVEN

THE SMASHERS

The referee placed the ball in the center of the field between Laura Rose and a big girl from Team Five. Laura Rose tried hard, but Team Five won the kick-off.

The ball went speeding toward the Comets' end of the field. Venus ran after it, along with the other Comets.

"Play your positions!" Mrs. Posner yelled.

The Comets piled up in front of their goal. Julie got to the ball and booted it away. It went to Keisha—and then back to Team Five. Everything was happening so fast. There was a blur of blue and orange pinnies.

"Venus! Jill!" Mrs. Posner yelled. "In your positions!"

Where was her position supposed to be, anyway? Carmen was the only one who had hung back. Venus moved to get in line with her. Carmen was on the left. Venus was on the right. It was awfully hard to wait for the action to come her way.

"Come on, Comets!" a mother yelled.

"Go, Smashers!" a father from the other side screamed.

So Team Five was the *Smashers!* That sounded kind of dangerous.

Jill S. got the ball away from a Smasher.

"Kick it, Jill!" a mother yelled.

"Stop her! Stop her!" a father on the other side yelled.

Jill kicked hard. The ball flew up the field. Venus ran for it. So did Carmen.

"I've got it!" Carmen yelled.

"I have it!" Venus yelled. She could almost taste her first goal!

Carmen and Venus crashed into each other. They both fell down. The ball skittered out of bounds.

"Blue!" called the referee.

Venus caught her breath while the action stopped.

Carmen glared at her. "That was *mine*," she said.

"I might have scored," Venus said.

Carmen narrowed her eyes. "I *would* have." Under her breath, she muttered, "Hot dogger!"

The throw-in by a Smasher rolled in front of another Smasher, but Julie managed to steal it. She kicked the ball and it flew to the right near the Smashers' end. Venus ran for it. Carmen came running from the left. Venus, gasping for breath, got there first. She dribbled toward the goal. Two Smashers blocked her.

"Hey, catch her hair," one of them said.

It wasn't fair to talk about the way she looked! Venus got madder and madder as she struggled to keep the ball. It wasn't fair to her or to Angie or to anyone!

"Get her in the knee," a Smasher yelled. "Get her bandage."

A big gap-toothed blonde kicked Venus's knee.

"Ow!" Venus stopped to grab her knee.

The other Smasher stole the ball from between Venus's feet. She sent it toward the Comets' goal. It went past Laura Rose and Jill M. Another Smasher trapped it. And then the kick. Angie, all flailing legs and arms, tried to stop it, but it went right past and into the goal!

The Smasher parents cheered.

Smashers 1, Comets 0.

Later, a Smasher got the ball away from Jill S. She kicked wild and the ball was loose. Keisha ran for it. She wasn't fast enough. A Smasher captured it and started up the side.

"Come on, defense!" Mrs. Posner yelled. "Block her, Julie, block her!"

Julie tried. But the Smasher brushed past her. The Smasher booted it at the Comets' goal.

Angie looked scared. She blinked as the ball

headed her way. She stretched for it, but it whizzed past her.

Smashers 2, Comets 0.

What a disaster! They were slicing right through the Comets.

At half-time, the Comets were sweating and out of breath. Venus had never run so much in her life. She was thirsty and her knee hurt. Oh good! Coach was handing out orange sections. Venus sucked the juice from hers. It ran down her chin.

"Listen, Venus," Carmen said. "I didn't mean that, calling you a hot dogger. It's just—well, with my brothers watching, I wanted to prove a *girl* can play, too."

Venus thought for a moment before she answered. "You were right. You would have scored."

Carmen shrugged. "Maybe."

Across the field, the Smashers were jumping around and giving each other high-fives. The Comets watched, their shoulders drooping.

"Angie's no good," Jill M. said. "Angie let them get two goals!"

"Yeah," Jill S. said. "The goalie's supposed to *stop* them!"

Angie tucked her head down and bit her lip.

"Leave her alone! It's not her fault," Venus said. "It went past *all* of us before it ever got to the goalie!"

Julie gave Venus a long look. "That's the truth," she said.

"Come on, everybody, let's pull together," Mrs. Posner said. "Pass to each other. Talk to each other out there. Carmen and Venus—you're on the same team, remember? Now go out there and turn it around!"

The teams changed sides. The second half just *had* to be better!

CHAPTER TWELVE

THE SECOND HALF

The Comets won the kick-off and Laura Rose passed the ball to Julie. She dribbled up the side with Smashers all around her.

"Kick it! Kick it hard!" a father shouted.

"Hold on to it, Julie! Center it!" a mother yelled.

The parents on the sidelines were screaming all different directions. Everything was confusion.

Mrs. P's voice cut through. "Pass to Venus!"

The ball flew to Venus. She trapped it. She had it! She dribbled toward the Smashers' goal.

"In the knee! Get her knee!" a Smasher yelled.

Oh no! The big blonde was bearing down on her.

But Carmen had heard. "That stinks," she muttered. She stopped the blonde.

Then Keisha, Laura Rose, and Julie were there, too, keeping Smashers away from Venus. She had friends here!

Venus headed toward the goal. If she scored, she'd be a soccer star! But could she aim her power kick from the side? She didn't know. Carmen had run to the center in line with the goal. Carmen would score for sure. That was important. The Comets were losing! Could she give up her chance to shine? No time to think.

Venus passed to Carmen.

Carmen trapped the ball and booted it. The Smasher goalie lunged for it, but it went in. It went in!

Smashers 2, Comets 1.

The Comets screamed and hugged each other.

Suddenly Venus heard a familiar voice, louder than all the rest.

"Yay, Venus! Yay, Venus!"

Mom had come! She was waving both arms in the air.

"Two more," Carmen said. "Let's do it."

The referee placed the ball for the kick-off. It flew way into Smasher territory. The big blonde got behind it and booted the ball the other direction, nearly to the goal. Julie got under it and let the ball bounce off her chest to stop it. It went from Comet to Smasher to Comet and back to Smasher again, up and down the field.

Venus saw Mom kicking the grass at her feet.

Carmen got the ball, but Smashers were all around her.

"Venus!" Carmen yelled as she passed it.

Venus trapped it. She dribbled up the side. None of the Smashers had caught up yet. She had a breakaway!

"Venus! Venus! Venus!" Mom was screaming.

Venus kicked and the ball whizzed toward the goal. But it hit the post and bounced back.

A Smasher had it and was kicking it toward the

other end. Carmen looked fierce as she got it away. She passed to Julie and ran back into position. Julie passed to Venus. A Smasher was zooming in on her. Venus passed to Carmen. Carmen dribbled up the side and let go. Another goal!

Smashers 2, Comets 2!

Everyone was jumping and giving high-fives. Keisha did a wriggly dance move. "One more, one more!" they chanted as they ran back into position.

The Comets worked hard for another goal, but the whistle blew first. Time up. The game was over.

The Comets were panting as they gathered around Mrs. Posner.

"Terrific second half," the coach said. "Good job!"

"We'll win the next one, Mrs. P," Keisha promised.

Mrs. Posner smiled. "Two beautiful goals, Carmen. And two assists for Venus. That was fine teamwork."

Venus grinned. She didn't know they gave credit for assists.

"Remember, everybody, practice on Monday," Mrs. Posner continued. "At four sharp."

"I'll be there!" Venus couldn't wait. She had made up her mind to practice every single day. She'd work on control. She'd learn to aim her kick the way Carmen could.

"Do you want to run with me tomorrow?" Angie whispered.

"Sure," Venus said. "I'll meet you at the track." She'd work with Angie, and they'd both get better. They'd win the next one for sure!

Both teams lined up in the middle of the field to shake hands.

Venus was in front of Julie.

"Two assists. That was great," Julie said.

Venus glowed. "Thanks." She couldn't help asking, "How come you're being nice to me all of a sudden?"

Julie shrugged. "Because . . . I don't know . . . because you've changed."

"Right." Venus tugged at odd wisps of her hair. "Because I'm not beautiful anymore."

"Like I care." Julie laughed. "You've still got the exact same face. It's just your hair, that's all. No—you've been *acting* different."

"How do you mean?"

"Like standing up for Angie. That was a nice thing to do."

"She's my friend."

"And pitching in with everybody else. And acting like a team player. Now *that's* a switch. I thought you'd only be out for yourself."

Venus looked straight into Julie's eyes. "I'm no hot dogger."

Julie stared back. "I'm no Jill-clone. I can talk to anyone I like."

"I'm not being different," Venus said. But maybe she was, a little. And maybe Julie was, too. The Jills might even turn out to be halfway human. Venus wouldn't bet on it.

After shaking hands—Venus had to shake that big blonde's hand!—the girls scattered.

Venus ran to Mom. "Did you see my assists? Did you?"

"You were *brilliant*," Mom said. "And only your first game. You must be *amazingly* talented."

"Carmen's the best on the team, but—"

Mom's eyes were shining. "Isn't there a soccer team in the Olympics? If we get a special coach and start training immediately—"

Venus's stomach knotted. "Mom, I don't want to get a special coach."

Mom went on. "You'll get endorsements and commercials. Maybe *sneakers!* Star athletes can—"

"Mom, don't! Please. *Listen* to me!"

"What? What do you mean?"

"I just want to play," Venus mumbled. "That's all."

"Oh." Mom bit her lip.

"And go to practice with my friends."

"Oh. Of course."

"Mom, I'm sorry. "

"No," Mom said. "You're right. Absolutely."

Venus felt bad for her. "I—I have to help my

team pick things up. Move the goals and stuff."

"I think you should." Mom adjusted Venus's sweatband over the little tufts of hair. Her hand touched Venus's cheek. "I guess I got a little carried away again. It *was* an exciting game."

"I'll be right back, Mom."

"Sure, go ahead. I'll wait here."

Venus took a few steps and then she turned back. "I can't help it. I want to be a regular kid for now. But when I grow up—"

"That's way far off. For now, I'll come to all your games and cheer for the Comets," Mom said, smiling. "I'll try not to cheer too much louder than the other mothers. Is that okay?"

"Okay!"

Venus gave her a huge smile back. And it wasn't the make-believe modeling kind. This one came right from her heart.

ABOUT THE AUTHOR

ERIKA TAMAR was born in Vienna, Austria, and was raised in New York City. After graduation from New York University, she worked in television production and as a casting director for a TV daytime serial. Her second career as a writer began in 1983 with the publication of her first book, a young adult novel. Since then, she has written twenty books: picture books, middle grade and young adult. Books by Ms. Tamar include *Alphabet City Ballet*, *The Junkyard Dog*, and *The Midnight Train Home*. Her many awards include the California Young Readers Medal, the Virginia Young Readers Award, ALA's Best Books for Young Adults, and the Spur Award for best juvenile from the Western Writers of America. Ms. Tamar lives in Manhattan, New York.